C000231069

Kurt Tucholsky
Rheinsberg

# Rheinsberg

## A Storybook for Lovers

### and

## Among City Wizards
## Love Poems for Claire

# Kurt Tucholsky

## Translated by Cindy Opitz

New York 2014

Rheinsberg
By Kurt Tucholsky

Translator: Cindy Opitz
Editor: Eva C. Schweitzer
Copy editor: Mark LaFlaur

© 2014 by Berlinica Publishing LLC
255 West 43rd St., Suite 1012
New York, NY, 10036, USA

ISBN 978-1-935902-25-6
LCCN: 2013956058

Photos pp. 14, 67, 78, 86: Kurt Tucholsky Museum
Photos pp. 60, 68: Kurt Tucholsky Society
Photos pp. 18, 23, 26, 31, 34, 39, 44, 49: Postcard from around 1900
Photos pp. 52, 57, 59, 84, 85: Eva C. Schweitzer
Cover photo: Historic postcard of the Rheinsberg Castle;
Image editing: Sue Yerou

Kurt Tucholsky Society: www.tucholsky-gesellschaft.de
Tucholsky Museum: http://www.tucholsky-museum.de

Printed in the United States

All rights reserved under International and Pan-American Copyright Law. No part of this book may be used or reproduced in any manner whatsoever without written permission except in the case of brief quotations embodied in critical articles and reviews.

www.Berlinica.com
http://blog.berlinica.c

*Love is when she brushes the crumbs from your sheets*
Kurt Tucholsky

# Contents

# Preface to the Fiftieth Thousand

## Kurt Tucholsky
### *Die Weltbühne*, December 8, 1921

*This is the preface Kurt Tucholsky wrote for* Die Weltbühne *after a special edition of* Rheinsberg *was published, on the occasion of 50,000 copies sold. We are republishing it here, slightly abridged.*

In *Börsenblatt*, the main trade publication for German book-sellers, I found an announcement: the publisher is celebrating 50,000 copies in print with a special commemorative deluxe edition of *Rheinsberg, a Storybook for Lovers*, signed by the author. The foreword, it claimed, was written by Kurt Tucholsky. But that isn't the right one. Where could I write something clever in an autographed deckle volume? The right foreword goes here:

Rheinsberg . . . *Et hoc meminisse iuvabit* . . . Back then, it went something like this: I wrote the book, later used for generations as a blueprint for love, by the seaside, bent over the page with Claire warming me at my side, and upon returning to Berlin read it aloud to the artist Szafranski. That was a delight! The chubby man said he'd never heard such a load of bullshit before in his life, but if I revised it a little and he illustrated it, it might be all right. I revised it, leaving out the nice parts, fleshed out the mediocre ones a bit, and he, meanwhile, illustrated it, because if a true rip-off artist is anything, he's industrious. While he was busy plagiarizing, I went to see Master Publisher Axel Juncker.

Publishers are not people. They just act like them. This one threw me and my book out.

After Master Publisher Juncker hastily informed me that lovers never speak to each other like that, however, he accepted it after all. It was entirely fine by him.

Szafranski, meanwhile, had not been idle. But he was nowhere near being done. We had long and downright unfriendly conversations on the telephone. Finally he asked me to meet him at the former "Queen Bar" and showed me what he had done. I downed four shots of whiskey in quick succession and timidly told him that it was quite beautiful. Szafranski, gullible as he is, believed it. The project went to press.

It was a huge success. I won't even mention my earnings; Szafranski, suffice it to say, used his share to buy himself something he passes off as a cottage among his circle of friends and is now considered one of the most respected citizens of Zehlendorf. The publisher did what publishers always do: he lost money.

We had opened up the "Book Bar" on Kurfürstendamm then, student nonsense that annoyed people half to death, because the shop had a polyglot sign in all languages, dead or alive—including mumbling—that cheap books were available within. The genteel clientele received schnapps. The press went beserk. *Breslauer Zeitung* was against it, whereas *Vossische Zeitung* endorsed it; Prague and Riga were neutral—we still have the clippings—and the *St. Petersburg Herald* wrote on December 18, 1912, that those who purchased a Wilde received a whiskey soda, and those who bought an Ibsen got a Nordic corn. But it wasn't true—we were the ones drinking. And we sold an awful lot of *Rheinsberg*s.

So we gave up the book bar, because a good joke is an

ephemeral one, and its time had passed. What Axel Juncker did with the book, meanwhile, was never known. Apparently he didn't like parting with it, because it was nowhere to be had. Szafranski thought it must have gone something like this: whenever anyone came into the bookstore and asked about the book, Juncker smiled smugly and inquired with concern, "Is that really necessary?" And when the odd customer insisted on pursuing his request, the publisher crept down to the cellar and retrieved the small volume from a well protected corner, but not without carefully dusting it off first. This last detail, however, proves that the story cannot possibly be true.

And in Radviliškis*, where we were teaching the German way to the world, they received word from the publisher that the first edition was out of print and—how he must have suffered!—now he would have to print a second. I expected to be called in front of the company and commended, but that did not happen. When I returned home—stabbed in the back—several thousand copies of *Rheinsberg* had sold. The publishing company had done all it could: for six months at a time, the adverse book, suitable for undermining the mood of the homeland, was out of print, because all paper was needed for the 1,001 army reports—but to Juncker's deepest regret the sale could not be entirely avoided. We didn't know a thing about royalties. I showed my contract, the first one I'd ever had in my life, to the chairman of the Association of German Authors. He cried joyful tears for half an hour and patted me gently on the head. To this day, I still don't know what he meant by that. And Juncker, meanwhile, kept losing money . . .

---

* Radviliškis was a town in Lithunia in the Baltics, where Tucholsky was stationed as a soldier in World War I.

Of course the story of *Rheinsberg* is true. And Claire still exists. She's a rickety, rheumy old woman living in Ducherow now, not far from Pasewalk, where the constable of city hall shows her off to curious visitors for a fee of twenty-five cents, from eleven to one and three to five. She's closed on Sundays. Her livelihood is graciously supported by our publisher, so she is utterly broke.

This is not the first deluxe edition. We had already made one, a private run when the book first came out. There were thirty copies—and because we had to give them to our ladies, in a ratio of 29:1 between us, we drew a nice "1" in every copy, to avoid any hard feelings.

Now we've grown old and just a little less handsome. Szafranski is married, and I've had my share of unhappiness in life, too; the publisher, though, is still losing money. Yet someday even we will have to take our leave—for beauty dies—Szafranski will be carried to his grave, the bosses he works for will puff him up a bit, his brother will give a speech and look really nice in his top hat, I'll plant some celery and little strawberries on his grave, which the departed always loved to eat; and then I'll go, too, following in his footsteps. And the publisher will go to heaven—indeed, it happens, no need to be so strict about it, with purgatory overflowing—and the stream of *Rheinsberg* copies still available will dry up, the pages will crumble, and then there will no longer be any more.

In 1985, however, when a curious and enamored young man is rummaging through his grandmother's bookcase, he'll pull out a signed volume on laid paper, bound in red buckskin, from way in the back—number 18, signed by the author. "What's this?" the young man will inquire.

And his grandmother will take the book, hold it up close to her eyes, and smile softly. "That," she will say, "is something your late grandfather once gave to me, when we got engaged. But you can keep it and give it to your Lydia." And the young man does just that. He packs up the buckskin book with a few things that are fashionable gifts at the time and sends it all to Lydia. And Lydia will be amazed by the fashionable things and delighted by them and by how envious her friends will be, and will take a look at the book, finally, and page through it a bit.

But because the clock is ticking and that which is written between the lines of a book doesn't last longer than fifty years and disappears with the people it was written by and for—because of this, Lady Lydia will shrug her shoulders and say, "How quaint!" and the story of her and the young man will continue.

And up in heaven, in an especially exclusive corner, right next to Cotta and Rowohlt, the publisher will still be sitting and losing money.

*Else Weil, on whom Tucholsky based Claire, the main character in his first novella,* Rheinsberg, *around 1912.*

# Rheinsberg

## A Storybook for Lovers

*Kurt Tucholsky, Charlottenburg, 1912*

*. . . it begins after sexual gratification, not beforehand. That is when souls unleash their full power, and not beforehand. That is when the battle unfolds in full glory, and not beforehand. That is when the characters stand on the same playing field, and not beforehand. Only then do the barriers between two people disappear, and not beforehand.*

Alfred Kerr

*Weary and bewreathed, summer lolls in the grass.*

Heinrich Mann

THE ADVENTURE only really began when they disembarked in Löwenberg. The long, dark express train rested under the station's wooden roof—they walked through a tunnel, up, into bright sunlight, where the local train waited, dainty and prim, as if made of wood.

They climbed aboard.

"Claire?"

"Wolfgang?"

"It looks like this train will be here for a while . . . should we take a little walk?"

"Sit down with your hands in your lap! It's about to leave."

The train shuddered and lurched its way past lettuce beds and courtyard walls. The horizon was a blinding white shimmer . . . Was this landscape a beauty? No—the groves of trees were unremarkable; distant hills concealed one little wood and revealed another—yet one could take general pleasure in the fact that it was all there . . . The little engine snorted and pinged irately, sounding melodic through the dusty smoke, like a church bell tolling in a storm.

"Wolf, the guidebook!"

They had left it on the express train—or rather he had left it on the express train.

They stopped along the way, in the middle of a forest. Heads out. The conductors ran back along the track with shovels in their hands. The locomotive must have thrown off sparks and started a small fire . . .

"I'm gonna help put it out!"

He rolled down the sandy bank; their fellow travelers laughed. Claire stood up above, rolling her eyes.

"Really?"

He returned, covered in dirt, smiling and happy. He had been active again. The conductors came, climbed aboard, and the train lurched on . . .

"Actually . . . "

"Hmmm?"

"It's funny. Just think, my Papa and Mama are sitting in the office or driving around town and think their dear daughter is safe and snug in the care of her devoted girl-friend. When actually . . . "

"When actually . . . ?"

"Well, you're the one looking after me . . . "

The hunter next to them had been snickering to himself for some time. He sat there, green, heavily laden, solid, and tanned. He brought to mind a damp early morning: a man groping around in the half-dark forest, it smells strong and good . . . The small, round hole in the muzzle of his rifle pointed sinisterly in the air, black and dark: tiny pellets will fly out, the deer at which it will point tomorrow might have been running to the spring with its mate that very moment, pausing for a drink, and disappearing gracefully into the woods . . . The hunter stood, filled his pipe, and said on his way out, "Closed season, young man, enjoy the honeymoon!" and tromped out with a laugh.

They filled the compartment with shouting, trying to be heard over the clanking and rumbling of the train.

It was difficult to make themselves understood:

" . . . sun high above the land . . . "

" . . . what? Sun nigh above the land?"

" . . . no . . . sun hiiiigh . . . land . . . Look, an acacia! An acacia in bloom! Look at all of the acacias in bloom!"

"Is not, that's a magnolia!"

"Hah! Which one of us knows more about botany? Me, or me?"

"It's a magnolia."

"My dear, I deeply regret that I cannot simply leave it at a hard punch to your gut. All of the characteristics of an acacia indicate that these trees, too, are those."

"But that's a magnolia."

"Good God, Claire! Don't you see the characteristically oval leaves, the small, white, bunchy blossoms? Wench!"

"But . . . Wolfie . . . where there's a magnolia . . . "

She was smothered in kisses.

Then at the last station they made like the farmer's wife, who stood and gathered up her skirts, legs spread wide, and blew her nose on her second petticoat. Claire proved to be adept and efficient at this.

And finally they arrived after all.

The hotel, which a placard on the train had touted as renowned and a source of fine cuisine, was represented

Rheinsberg, Fernblick auf das Schloss

*Rheinsberg Castle in Brandenburg, shown in a postcard from around 1900.*

by a carriage, two horses, and a servant. The latter went to fetch the luggage they had so carefully checked in Berlin: two teeny-tiny suitcases. These were loaded onto the carriage, and the travelers climbed aboard. They slid around on their seats on black, oilcloth pillows that were losing their stuffing in places; the windows clattered, and the couple communicated with elaborate hand gestures. The carriage was empty, and the country road dusty and desolate. For a few hundred yards they were well behaved, but by the time they reached the corner formed by the post office and the Johannes Lauterbach estate, they were bickering loudly about whose suitcase's small size would arouse the most suspicion. They called these travel articles "canvas piggies," and Claire was wringing her hands because Wolf was an eyesore. She, for her part, was the picture of decorum. They squabbled incessantly, Claire the most fiercely. Her language was not conventional. She had a manner of speaking that was principally reminiscent of the idiom of small children trying to establish their first vocal associations with their environment; she swirled the words around until they were barely recognizable, left out a "g" here and added an "s" there, mixed up all her articles, and no one ever really knew whether she meant to make fun of the inadequacy of a phrase or make fun of others. It was hard to believe that she was a doctor, as she claimed to be and which was, indeed, consistent with reality. She was always playful, always bringing some real or imagined figure to life for a few moments . . .

The carriage came to a halt. As they climbed out, Wolfgang said, "Look out, little woman, where's the suitcase with the counterfeit dough? Ah, there . . . "

The servant's jaw dropped and his eyes grew wide . . .

The old innkeeper cheerfully led them to a room on the second floor. It was simple, sparse, and papered in flowers. It contained wooden beds, a large washstand, and a vase with a bouquet of artificial flowers—two decorative pieces hung on the wall: "The Norman Invasion of England," and, in the same style of frame and symmetrically hung, "Grandpa's 70th Birthday." The door closed, and they were alone.

"Claire?"

"Wolfgang?"

"I'm not sure, but I might've left the key to the suitcase at home . . . "

"My honey-suckle," and she kissed him firmly on the mouth, with a vicious, vindictive gleam in her eye, and pushed him away. "Oh, the widdle bitty boy is always forgetsing—tsk, tsk, tsk . . . " And it was hard to tell whether the tone was meant to mimic a soothing mother or something entirely different.

"Time to unpack, my sweetie pie!"

Sighing heavily, they unpacked and settled in.

"Well, now I's done. I'll coif my hair and then go walkin's. An' you?"

"You just leave that to me; you'll be informed of any necessary details in due time."

Their style, generally speaking, was consistently distorted. They often said things to each other that didn't really fit together, just to be able to use this or that expression, to irritate each other, throw each other off balance . . . They went downstairs . . .

To the town square, planted with old, low-growing trees, shady and silent. They stepped through a wrought-iron gate into the park. It was peaceful there. A workman hammered inside the plain, white walls of the castle. They went through the courtyard and back to the park, back to the silence . . .

The noise of the big city still hummed and thrummed inside them, the streetcars, conversations that had not yet died away, the noise of their journey here . . . the noise of their daily lives, no longer audible to them, but something their nerves had yet to overcome, which took a certain amount of their vital energy without them noticing . . . But there was a stillness here; the quiet had a debilitating effect, like when a steady, long-familiar sound suddenly ceases. For a long while they did not speak, allowing themselves to be soothed by the shady paths, the still surface of the lake, the trees . . . Like all big-city folks, they were amazed beyond measure by a simple shrub, overestimated its beauty and, without suspecting the practicality of all the rural circumstances surrounding them, they saw things perhaps as one-sidedly as the farmer, just from the other side. Here in Rheinsberg, objects did not require all that much practical knowledge; they weren't on some estate that needed administering, after all. They came to the edge of a second lake, a bench, silence . . .

"Wolfgang?"

"Claire?"

"D'ya think there's bearses here? An old aunt of mine was once nearly . . . "

" . . . mauled by a bear?"

"No." She was utterly indignant. "Did I say that? I only meant . . . But you, you'll protects, me, won't you?"

"I promise . . . "

"Hmm."

The silence returned. Claire sat and looked intently into the dirty green water.

"Say, why isn't that Freddy the Second all over the place around here? Like he's all over in Sanssouci. Along every path, in every grove, behind every statue? He lived here, didn't he? If you didn't know, you wouldn't notice."

"No. Maybe you have to be older or more powerful to fashion the world around you in your own image . . . Is there anyone today like Old Freddy was? Do our living rooms all look like they could belong only to their owners and no one else? . . . A woodpecker, do you see it? A woodpecker!"

"Wolfie, that's no woodpecker. That's a barn owl."

He stood up. With emphasis. "I have an extraordinarily fine feel for such things; I'm getting the feeling that you're determined to make fun of me. If this impression proves correct, I'll strike you down."

Her laughter carried far through the spruce trees.

The castle! They must see the castle. Their footsteps reverberated throughout the courtyard. They pulled on a brass rod with a porcelain knob. A tiny bell sounded. A window opened. "Be right there!" A door at the top of the small staircase opened; nothing came out; then there was some fumbling, and the massive castellan emerged in the courtyard. When he caught sight of the pair, he did something surprising. He introduced himself. "My name is Mr. Adler. I'm the castellan here." The pair thanked him graciously and presented themselves as the married Gambetta couple from Lindenau. The fat man seemed moved by past remembrances; his lips twitched, but he held his tongue.

"Come around back here, now; that's the closest . . . "

And unlocked a door made of wooden boards, which led to a dark stone stair. They trudged up the steep steps. At the top, in a former anteroom, brown felt slippers lay scattered on the floor, in every size, for large and small, twenty, thirty—it brought to mind some fairy tale in which a fairy had spilled them there, or a magic pot had malfunctioned once again and overflowed . . .

Claire asserted that there was no one that small.

"Eh," Mr. Adler said, "Just slip them on; it's all right if they're a little roomy; that don't matter."

Direkt am See.  Grosser schattiger Park.  Bequeme Bootsunterkunft.  40 Logierzimmer.

*Above: The Hotel Fuerstenhof, where Tucholsky and Else Weil stayed in Rheinsberg. Below: The hotel courtyard around 1900.*

He was not required to put on such shoes, however, because he wore felt slippers since birth.

The rooms through which he led them were sparsely and austerely furnished. Chairs stood rigidly upright against the walls. There were no subtle irregularities to make a room seem even remotely livable; everything stood at right angles here . . . Mr. Adler was explaining, " . . . and this here is the so-called prince's room, and the greyhound slept in this basket. The greyhound—you know what that is, yes . . .?"

"Just think, Claire, someday some silver-tongued guide will lead lovers through your rooms . . . "

"Thank God! He sure could! Our joint was classy."

And then Mr. Adler pointed out the Chinese vases, the very same ones that the young Count Schleuben had brought back from his trip to Asia.

But this—they entered another, superior room—this was the art gallery. The paintings were by Pesne, the famous artist, and they were so exquisitely done that their eyes followed the honored visitors' every move. Just give it a try! Mr. Adler revealed each fact one at a time, like a secret. It almost seemed as if he were continually surprised that his words didn't make a bigger impression on the visitors. Good God, Claire! She had begun asking the castellan questions. Wolfgang tried to stop her, but it was already too late.

"Tell me, Mr. Adler, how do you know all of this, about the castle and such?"

Mr. Adler traced his knowledge back to his predecessor, Mr. Breitriese, who got his in turn from Brackrock, who was archivist at the time.

"And then, I'm curious, Mr. Adler, did there use to be a bathroom here?"

"No, but we have one downstairs, if you're interested . . . "

They expressed their thanks. Mr. Adler, who had ended

by pointing out a miniature, a present from Grand Duchess Sofie of Russia, suddenly fell silent. Only after the tip was jingling in his fist did he look out the window and say somewhat absentmindedly, "This is a venerable castle the memory of which you will treasure forever. The sundial in the garden is also worth seeing."

Claire couldn't resist giving Wolf a little pinch as they walked out into the open, past the castellan's apartment, which smelled deliciously of cauliflower.

That afternoon, they rode around on the lake. He rowed, and she sat at the rudder, threatening now and then to make her old, gray family unhappy by jumping into the water, she was so fed up. He would capsize them any minute now, anyway. Instead they landed on a small island, where a couple of trees grew. They settled down on the grass . . . A cool breeze was blowing off the lake. The shoreline curved gently into the distance, the light blue surface shone softly . . .

"Looky, my l'il monkey, that there's your homeland. Tell me, would you go to your death for it?"

"You have it in writing, dear wife, that I'll only go to my death for you. Don't confuse the terms. *Amor patriae* is not the same as *amor* per se. They are completely different sentiments."

"Now I am content."

And, after long daydreams in the bright sky—it was so bright that twinkling sparks danced before their eyes when they gazed into it a long while—"Wolfie, you neverhow loved anyone else before me, did you?"

"Never!"

It was titillating to make light of the bourgeois folks' longing, of what they called love, of their craving to always be the first . . . Neither of them was inexperienced.

*Above: Rheinsberg Castle. Below: The bedroom of Prince Henry of Prussia, 1726-1802, in the castle. In 1786, it was suggested to Alexander Hamilton that Henry become King of the United States.*

Voices approached, rowboats, families wanting to land there for a picnic. Giant tin baskets filled with provisions threatened the peaceable folk like artillery . . . Up and away!

In the middle of the lake, "See thar, you gotta let me have rowed some too! Me wanna do dat too—boo."

"Go ahead, row!"

They changed places; the boat rocked.

Claire rowed. She was delighted. Once she lost both oars. He had to row with a stick. They finally caught the oars again, which had drifted a long way away.

"I can do it really well. I could even do it without oars— yes I could! Don't laugh, you rascal! Wasn't I right, pre-haps—ha!"

And rowed until she was huffing and puffing, like a little asthmatic steam engine. The sun was already setting by the time they reached the shore.

He paid. Claire chatted with the mistress of boat rentals. He heard, "So, quite a mighty breed here in these parts, eh?"

"Well, dearie, we beat up the guys pretty well ourselves!"

They laughed all the way to the hotel.

What a peaceful evening it was; they sat under the dark, low trees and waited for their food.

"Claire?"

"Wolfgang?"

"I'm so . . . "

"So good, my boy."

"No! All joking aside, there's something wrong with my stomach."

"That's cholera. Wait until you've had something to eat."

"No, listen—I've got this feeling, so empty, so . . . "

"Typical, That's just—characteristic, that is. You're dying, Wolfie."

"That's not the right kind of love on your part, either!

First I let you study medicine and now you won't even take a look through your stethoscope."

"My God, right—what's the meaning of this? Right? Whosoever . . . "

But she went along to the pharmacy after all, which was light brown and entirely modern and functionally equipped. White tins and porcelain pots lined the shelves, and a light scent of valerian could be detected throughout the premises. After a detailed consultation and genial conversation, the sick man received a small bottle filled with a dark brown liquid. It helped. Thank God.

Then they ate, and Claire had a smoke after the meal. Over by the house sat the men who all of the newcomers took for dignitaries. Lawyers, officials, and the pharmacist, whose breach of professional confidence regarding the visit of the couple elicited laughter from the small group.

"Cheers, Wolf, to the old folks!"

"To the old folks!"

Their glasses clinked, and the guests dining at long tables along the brightly lit house looked over at them. Claire blew smoke rings.

"What excessive impudence!" she decided.

"Hmm?"

"Coming here. What if no one notices? And no one will notice—you'll see, no one will notice."

"*Ne quis animadvertat!* Cheers!"

"You know, I'd rather travel with a flea circus as with you."

"'Than,' Claire, 'than with you.'"

"My God, couldn't ya have hads been in the habit of not better correcting me? I'm speaking the sheer standard!"

"Hmm. Those in the know sing cantatas to it. Would you like more to drink?"

"Would I like whom to drink? Nah."

"I find we should walk a bit, eh?"

They wandered through the dark town. After a long, black row of houses, they came upon an arc lamp surrounded by buzzing brown specks—insects desperate to enter the light.

"Claire?"

"Wolfie?"

"The creatures up there, do you see them?"

"Yes."

"Just like people."

She stopped walking.

"How so . . . please?"

"Like all living th . . ."

"Please—whatever there is to symbolize here, I'll symbolize for myself. You have to go to bed anyway. You're talking downright . . . different. Shall I pull your widdle leggie?"

"Paramour!"

They passed dark, shuttered windows and long walls; families sat behind red-lit curtains, playing cards . . . At one point they went into a courtyard, stumbled over the cobblestones, and looked through a window into an auditorium.

There was a play going on.

They could only see a small, yellow corner of light, but they could hear everything. "Ha ha," an overly loud woman's alto voice said, "We'll have to ask my brother-in-law about that. Oh, here he comes . . ."

The audience wheezed and twitched in the dark like some multiheaded beast. Shoulders moved. Heads turned this way and that . . .

"Heavens, there's Fritz," someone shouted on the stage, and the crowd of theatergoers laughed, their bodies bobbing up and down, some murmuring . . .

"How strange," Wolfgang said. "Outside it's silent as death, the moon is shining, and inside they're acting out a mock-life. We come along, not knowing anything about the situation in the first act, and remain earnest."

It was quiet; the brightly illuminated corner of the stage remained empty; someone must have made a funny gesture, because the women laughed shrilly and the men grunted approvingly. They leaned in closer and had a blurry view of the rest of the stage, distorted by the windowpane, which appeared to be a room with yellow wallpaper and painted furnishings. A man in a green apron was conversing with a stout female character in her forties. An old beach chair canopy served as the prompter's box. The couple heard the two say, "So, he's supposed to be cleaning"—the man was, in fact, holding a broom—"but instead he's bowing and scraping with the girls! He should watch out, the skirt chaser!" The audience giggled. "I'll rain on his parade. Here and here and there and there!"

The audience laughed, "Ha ha!" and the man, who until then had inclined his head to listen keenly in well-played foolishness, received a few slaps in the face . . . At that moment, a young girl stepped onto the stage, and the audience's amusement rose to such a frightening degree that the couple involuntarily stepped back from the window.

"The first act!" he sighed. "We don't have the first act!"

"Such a little boy, wants a look-see at the theater! Off to bed with you!"

And they left.

As they climbed the stairs, they heard lingering laughter from the animated dignitaries.

"Claire, are those land-cultivating citizens making fun of us? I am fearsome in my rage."

"Indeed, my widdle boy. Now off to bed."

Their large, broad-shouldered shadows danced on the wall as the candle flame danced . . . Claire stood before the mirror and let down her hair.

Rheinsberg.    Säulengang mit der Figur des Apollo.

*Postcard view of the lake from the Rheinsberg Castle courtyard,
with a statue of the Greek god Apollo.*

"Wolfie, listen; when I was yet a wee girl, I went to see my friend Alice—pick up my pin, will you!—and there was a man, I don't remember his name, and he said my hair was like spun silk. Yes he did."

"Yes, and?"

"Nahthin'."

Claire loved to tell pointless stories about simple occurrences from her childhood. She insisted that people listen to them often and became irate when they suggested they had already heard them.

"You're not friendly to me at all. You don't love me anymore."

Like an emotional chameleon, she took on a lovelorn demeanor. Her mouth was twisted in grief, her upper body slightly bowed, hands clenched.

"I, for one, am lying in bed," he said. The candle went out . . .

The pub clientele gossiped below. The proprietor could be heard making his rounds. "So, is our dear sister well again?–Yes, yes, I'm fine. Was everything all right? Yes . . . "

Upstairs, however, Claire said thoughtfully, slowly, "I'd like ta take youse and throw you in someone's goulash. Wouldn't he be surprised, right?"

But then she fell silent.

During the night, he woke up. He carefully smoothed the white, wrinkled curtain that was blowing softly in the night breeze. The moon haunted the trees, where an obelisk leaned menacingly, casting sharp shadows. The leaves rustled. Why do we react as if that's something beautiful, he mused. It's just a noise transmitted by sound waves . . . And proceeded to submissively surrender to the quiet rustling, which was a little sad but forebode great things and cleared one's chest . . . He spun around. A sleepy, childish voice said through a waterfall of hair, "Is there no one in my widdle bed, when there should be someone there, and widdle Claire is all alone . . . ?

He carried her back to bed.


When he returned from the barber early the next morning, Claire was just getting up. It went something like this: for the first fifteen minutes, she maintained a delicately murmuring stream of charming babble, disjointed syllables, and to flaunt a wide variety of animal imitations. He had just closed the door behind him when he was greeted by the mewing of a newborn kitten.

"Get up, Claire! Time to get up! Everyone is down at breakfast already."

A bit of exaggeration was necessary, or it was no use.

"Boo!"

"Yes, I know. Come on!"

He pulled off her blanket.

Later: "Wolfie, should I wear the green one or the white one?"

"Hmm, which one would you like to wear?"

"I . . . I don't know. *C'est pourquoi* I'm asking you."

"So wear the white one."

"Fine. This boy is so domineering, it's unspeakable. Ugh!"

Pause.

"Wolfgang?"

"Claire?"

"Do you really think I should wear the white one? Look . . . I mean, with the stains an' such . . . "

"So wear the green one."

"Fine."

A little while later: "Yes, but, uh, I'd really rather . . . "

"What would you rather?"

"The green one . . . "

Kurt Tucholsky

*Postcard view of the obelisk in the castle park;*
*Rheinsberg Castle in the background.*

"But that's what I said, wear that one!"

"Right, but . . . it's no fun when you tell me like that. You have to say, 'Don't wear it,' is what you have to say, or 'well, wear the white one.'"

And before he'd had a chance to recover, she let loose a marvelous tirade in the style of certain women who believe they've been insulted and make no bones about their feelings, even to the maid. The whole thing wasn't really suited to the situation, but she was on a roll, and there was no stopping her.

"Really? No one talks to me like that in my house, no one! You will not be dusting my expensive silk furniture, you . . . creature! When my husband, the mine assessor . . . "

He fled. Even out in the corridor, he could hear her whistling like a cobbler's boy.

The sun shone on the breakfast table; it smelled strongly and bucolically of milk, butter, and fresh-washed table-cloths. Bees and fat flies were swimming in an old honey jar that the proprietor had the forethought to fill with sugar water.

She came downstairs; neither said anything for a while. She ate . . . my God, she ate with the morning hunger typical of a late-sleeper.

"Claire?"

"Wolf?"

"I think we should go for a ride this morning."

"And what about me? He won't take me along at all! I want to go too!"

"I said 'we.'"

"Boo hoo!"

"Yes, you can come too. Now stop cryin' and eat."

"Wolfgang, your language isn't all that great either; no, you can't say that. But never fear, my efforts will get me to my goal."

She could speak very selectively, like old teachers some-times do, exaggerating the end syllables and palatal r's way back in the throat.

"My Papa always says, Wolfsie, that I don't speak very well. What? Yes, he's an experienced old man, but how does it befit him to speak—'Don't butt horns with levity, my child, and don't make light of such grave things!' I ask you, is he wrong or is he wrong? There are only two pos-sibilities to consider."

"He's right. There's the carriage."

He'd been lucky, because she had already risen to her feet and was standing there with her hands pressed firmly on the table, fixing him with a cross-eyed glare . . .

The carriage rolled light and fast along the green avenue.

"Wolfgang?"

"Claire?"

"Do ya notice sumpthin'?"

"What?"

"I aksed if ya notice sumpthin'."

"No."

"Well, take a lookie to me!"

"Nothing, by God. Shrugs his shoulders."

"You're not supposed to say what's in parentheses. 'Shrugs his shoulders,' that's in parentheses, you know?— But do you notice anything?"

"You washed your face."

"Ha! But . . . I wore a blue ribbon beneath my shirt yes-terday, but no more. You won't let me. Not you."

Did she not bear the look of one visibly aggrieved, call-ing upon the better emotions of her beloved with a pout?

"You gotta friend what says only waitresses wear color-ful ribbons in their underwear! Coulda told your friend, he coulda be'd with me, see'd if maybe I was a waitress."

Yes, he should arrange that.

But for now, all they could do was look out at the green landscape moving by. It wasn't like these woods possessed that glorious beauty we occasionally see in paintings and postcards. It didn't reveal any "divisions" or insights. But it made them happy. Or maybe it was simply their general joy at being alive. Between those who had come before them and those yet to be—now it was their turn—hooray! At a curve in the road, the coachman stopped, mumbled something, and disappeared in the brush. Claire accompanied his absence with pious speeches . . . And then they drove on, stopping to rest at a tavern on the lake, where they had a bite to eat.

Afterward, they took long detours on the way back to Rheinsberg. They came across pedestrians, sweating fathers with their jackets dangling from the end of walking sticks hoisted over their shoulders like rifles, silently yearning for the next beer tap; lovers stumbling along, hands entwined; once they heard part of a conversation between two sharp-tongued ladies.

"Yes," one of them said, "and to think she's a Berliner, but, you know, in the good sense of the word . . . "

The carriage jogged and clattered along, the horses clip-clopping awhile, then trudging slowly for a bit with lowered, nodding heads . . . And whenever they liked, they could lean back "on the canopy," as Claire called it, and gaze at the clouds, just the clouds, while their bodies moved pleasantly with the rhythm of the ride . . .

They arrived late in the afternoon; it was hot; maybe there would be a thunderstorm that evening, the proprietor said. They strolled into the park. At a small round flower bed, white figurines shimmered among the foliage. A satyr leaned against a tree stump, flute lowered, a faun nipped at a fleeing nymph . . . The castle radiated white, the windowpanes sparkled violet in their bright frames, dabbed with pink from dusty lamps, everything mirrored in the smooth surface of the water. Clumps of trees stood by, shining reddish yellow with black shadows, casting long, dark patches on the lawn. For a while, the lake pushed lazily against the reedy shore . . .

"Boiling hot. Can you get heatstroke from something like this, Claire?"

She lay on the ground, chewing on a bobbing stem that sprang up from her mouth.

"That depends entirely on your internal temperature, my boy. You—as hot as you are—yes, you can get sunstroke! Show me your tongue—hmmm . . . "

"You should've paid more attention to your lectures, instead of carving hearts with your initials in the benches. That women should study at all . . . "

"Please have a seat." She was utterly dignified, and although she was sitting in the grass, one might have believed from the expression on her face that she was a very busy doctor very interested in her patients.

"We'll find a road to recovery, yes we will . . . "

She stroked an imaginary beard. "Do you know whether your grandfather ever suffered from *icterus katarrhalis*? Or *angina vincentis*? We'll soon remedy this malady. Would you please open your mouth, wider, wider—so . . . " And she shoved the attentive patient backward, into the grass . . .

The air lay unmoving, oppressive around them; they crossed a bridge, beneath which flowed green, slimy water. They looked down. Leaves floated by, small twigs, bits of wood . . .

"Wolfgang?"

"Claire?"

"Can I, please? Just once, pretty please?"

She pressed against him, nuzzling him, buttering him up, so to speak . . .

"What, what is it, child?" He freed himself from her embrace.

*Above: A view of the Hotel Furstenhof from the lake.*
*Below: A public beach along the lake.*

"Lemme, please? Never did'ya lemme whom! I really, reeeaallllly wanna . . . "

"But what?"

She fell silent. They went back to watching the water flow away from the bridge.

"Wolfgang," Claire said wistfully, "Just once I'd like to spit in the water . . . " And in her highest voice, "Will you allow it?" Then squeaking, "Yes?"

He allowed it.

They walked through the streets of the city. Shop windows offered their enticing wares, artfully arranged. Oh, this was the absolute pinnacle, as one might say with pride; this was a place where the achievements of the new era were at hand: a modern wind was blowing here. Mr. Krummhaar, the owner of the delicatessen on the corner of the market square, for example, had arranged his window in accordance with artistic principles. Upon looking through his brightly polished window, the observer was treated to a paradisaical landscape: atop a bread-crumb hill stood a sugar loaf with a red gelatin cross, and upon closer examination one discovered that it was a windmill; plum paths wound their way around beds of currants with price tags; and a brig floated on a mirror, carrying bulbous bottles of Danziger Goldwasser and pretzels from faraway India . . . By the shop door, there were stacked containers filled with expensive peas and all manner of dried fruits, though they appeared to have gathered much dust; only those who were well informed might have recognized it as a subtle trick. For a long while, Claire stood gazing at the colorful splendor, then shivered, saying, "And an ox, fully loaded with meat extract . . . "

She stopped everywhere, wanted to buy everything, and she twirled around, chattering, laughing, and was a woman trying to get her man to shop, a disobedient whiny child dragged through the street by its nursemaid, a small dog—one after the other—and for ten paces, she even mimicked a not entirely irreproachable creature . . .

In front of the door of a small shop whose window promised linens and trims, the Mistresses Luft stood, two sweet-tempered elderly characters who smelled a little musty . . .

They were enjoying the evening air during a break between customers. They coaxed the pair into their shop.

"I would like some lingerie buttons, please." Claire was all business, right on task.

"Tsk . . . "

"Please, give me some white buttons, please . . . to sew onto things . . . "

"Tsk . . . of course."

Neither Miss Luft made any move, but merely stared at each other and the visitors, who practically filled their shop, perplexed and confused. One of them took a deep breath . . .

"Vould the joung sire step out for a moment? . . . "

*What a decent soul,* he thought. And left.

"A cinematograph? Here in Rheinsberg? Wolfie, after dinner? Yes?"

Really, there was one, and they went.

Along the way, the clouds started rumbling, gathering slowly. Wind shook leaves off the rustling trees, and dust swirled in the air . . .

Yet they were still dry when they arrived at the hall in the tavern. Right, a small orchestra was there; the room darkened . . .

NATURE! PICTURESQUE RIVER-
CRUISE THROUGH BRITTANY.
COLORIZED.

The chattering apparatus projected a smoky beam of light through the hall. A colorful landscape appeared, multi-colored, gaudy, and bright. The colorization was true to nature: the trees were spinach green, the sky swimming in pink and blue in eternal dusk . . . While the bright riverscape passed brightly by, a black shadow flickered constantly in the picture, suggesting that the recording was made from the deck of a steamship. This proved to be true; after a while, the light brown deck planks of a ship swung into view, which now included things nearby as well as off in the distance: a woman dressed in pink with a white lace parasol, apparently procured for just such an occasion, whose friendly smile, waving, and strolling up and down the deck generated an atmosphere of summer bliss; behind her, the colorized elements of Brittany glided by, weeping willows with branches drooping into the water, small yellow-ochre cottages whose color seemed to have bled into their surroundings, a passing trawler . . .

Claire sat there, shaken.

"Wolfgang, it's too sad! D'ya think the dying soldier will ever reach his homeland?"

He didn't think so. All the less, now that the pianist who'd just arrived played three mighty, noisy chords, knocked over his beer glass, yet managed to compose himself enough to accompany the next film, "Moritz Learns to Cook," in an appropriate manner. The music frolicked: The neighbor sticks his head in the door, Moritz is standing at the stove, grabs the other, stuffs him in the pot with his legs sticking out. Swaying, falling, pots overturning, flood, swimming down the stairs together, shaking hands at the bottom, sticks the dripping furniture under his arm and disappears . . .

Claire could not calm down: she kept asking questions, wanting to know everything. Did he know how to cook now, was the neighbor well done, she could cook, by the way, perfectly, she was just saying . . .

And didn't stop until bright letters on a dark background announced:

"The Rescue Light"
Starring Mr. Violo
From the Royal Opera House in Greiz

By unspoken, friendly agreement between the film company and the audience, the color blue signified night, and red a catastrophic blaze, so it became clear to everyone how much the groom's rescue light was needed at such a dangerous hour. Despite the transparent plot, life was concentrated here. When the ocean, the surf broke on the cliffs, when the courtyard of a house appeared clearly for a moment and you could tell from the branches how the wind was blowing, the moment was gone, irretrievably gone . . . How frighteningly beautiful it was when railway trains drew ever closer, ever larger, like giant shadows—a head looking out a window . . .

But when the luminous figures began to cry and a pump organ began to play, Claire sighed and expressed with a sob the desire to go home . . .

They battled wind and rain all the way back to the hotel.

The next morning, they walked to the fields. A chill had arrived with yesterday's storm; the first days of fall had arrived. The wind blew hard. As they walked against the wind, it wailed as if in mourning . . . Frothy piles of leaves lined the pathways. Milky white light glazed the fields. The sun hid behind stormy clouds, occasionally peeking out, red and frozen in the raw, robust autumn air. An empty path lay before them, swept clean by the wind—and it was bliss, walking along it; young linden trees stood in endless rows, and it was nice having the creaking trunks by their

*Postcard view of the Market Place in the town of Rheinsberg.*
*Below: The lake with the Miralonda mansion (right).*

side. Their breath was deep, their shoulders raised high. They walked in lockstep.

Longing—longing for fulfillment! Everything was here (he thought), autumn, the clear, clarifying autumn, Claire, everything—and yet they were drawn farther, their feet striving forward, toward some goal somewhere, never to arrive!

Much, almost everything on the planet could be satisfied, nearly every longing fulfilled—just not this one. What, when observed from above, was a lover?—A fool. When his beloved opened her heart to him, he was silent, sated and content. Entire literatures would not exist if girls unbolted their doors . . . An amoroso could be satisfied—give him the wife he desires, and his sonorous voice falls still. What might make us fall silent? We have nothing left to conceal, we've discovered all of our bodies' secrets . . . and our souls'? There are words that must remain unspoken, lest they die . . . But we don't want to delve these depths of the treasure chamber, we have each other completely and yet we're filled with longing. What is it that drives us onward, further, higher, forward? It isn't spring, because it's there in every season; it isn't youth, because we feel it at every age; it isn't Claire, we feel it anyway.

They came upon a windless grove of young birches.

To be happy, but never satisfied. Never letting the fire be extinguished, never ever! Sluggish, black, foul water swirled in a round hole. Everything else is a prelude: courtship, permission, indulgence. Then it begins and never ends. But what comes before? Occupied with the simple question: Yes? No? Do they not see what is essential, actual, strip what is yours from your desire to own her, put her in your room, contented, alone, think, you have everything you wanted . . . Would she stay? Can she promise more than allure? Can she give? Not everyone makes it through this test of endurance. It isn't for naught that one fearfully watches over the last one, not knowing that it's the dearest thing one has to give. Conquests by which the appeal lies solely in the conquest. Yet we strive to own.

And there is no deeper longing than this: the longing to be fulfilled. It cannot be satisfied . . .

"Wolfie! Hello!" She had wandered far ahead and was picking white serviceberries in the bushes, placing them in a circle on the ground and cracking them open with her foot.

"Why are you doing that?"

"Have you no sense of beauty? Do you not feel that it's satisfying, a release, as if from a pressure, when the berry . . . finally . . . cracks open . . . philistine!"

The grass glistened in the light; a fat beetle wandered across the path and took flight; the wind carried the beetle away; was he floating there? He'd be just as happy there, too . . .

A herd of sheep scampered across the stubbly fields; they wanted to move out of its way, but it was too late; a sheepdog had barked a long row into place, and they were in the middle of it; the sheep surrounded them, with Claire laughing and swaying in the sea.

"Wolfie, what if the animals eats me?"

"Not you, Miss, it wouldn't be worth it."

Finally they crawled out, laughing and covered in dust.

"How you found your way out, Wolfie!"

They were in an open field; the green grass waved, gleaming, in the wind; the air was moving swiftly, but the land lay calm, let it blow and pass over it; the earth remained firm.

They stood on a small hill, the land spreading like waves, far into the distance; the strong breeze playfully tugged at their hair. To be able to embrace all of this, not because it is good or beautiful, but because it's there, because the cloud banks are white and fluffy, because we're alive! Vigor! The vigor of youth!

"Claire?"

"Hmm?"

And was grabbed and carried away like a babe in arms, down the hillside and into a deep crater in bloom.

And arrived back in Rheinsberg again, and because it was their last day, Wolf disappeared and came back before lunch with a large, white package. Arriving upstairs, he laid it on the table. Claire was at the mirror, tugging at her hair. She turned.

"Wolfgang?"

"Claire?"

"What's this?"

"Nahthin', as you like to say."

"But, well . . ."

"To avoid any further debate, my dear woman, I hereby declare with raised voice that while there is something in this package, you, however, will not be permitted to open the same, with emphasis, before this evening. The train leaves at ten; at a quarter to, you may. Period."

"Hmm."

Pause.

"Wolfgang?"

"Claire?"

"Lemme me know what's in dere? Look . . ."

"Silence. I have spoken."

"But Wolfie, I think you can tell me the beginning letters and the ones in back, I mean the ending letters, right?"

"I will shatter you. No."

"Just the beginning, yeah? Pretty please!"

"Enough. We're going to eat!"

There was quite a "spread"—"There's soups," argued Claire, who knew everything, "an' henny-goose with vegetables and roots (roots? Fruit, Wolfie, fruit), an' then thar's . . . wanna know, Wolfie?"

"Yes."

"Hmm. I'll tell you. But first you have to tell me what's in the package . . . "

"I don't want to know."

"Boo!"

She threw a tantrum worthy of a small child and stuck out a Habsurg lip until the food arrived.

"Wolfie, does one eats soup with a knife?"

"What?"

"Well, I saw someone once, who eated with a knife."

"Soup?"

"No-oh-oh . . . "

An older woman limped past their table, squinted, and muttered something about "unheard of" and "person" and such.

"Wolfie, she means me. Couldn't you have had done challenged her? I am pretty refined, ain't I? Or d'ya think I'm a prostitute? No-o. Am not. Not I. Huh?"

"Let's defer to her age, my child. Maybe she doesn't have any fond memories of her youth . . . What did the great Frederick write in the margin of his files? 'My dear privy councilors,' he wrote, 'we're old and can't anymore; let's be happy for those who can'."

And then they ate, and when it was over: "Wolfie, the sun is shining so beautifully; let's take a photo!"

They retrieved their camera, which took a while to set up. It was to be a timed exposure, under the leafy canopy of the old trees, which allowed dappled light through to the ground below.

"Now you stand there, Wolfie. Listen, we'll makes a long exposure. You gotta stand absoludably still, got it? Totally still; I'll go away, meantime, so's I don' make you laugh . . ."

*Postcard views of the Rheinsberg Castle park around 1910;*
*the sphinx stairway (above) and the pavilion (below).*

He stood stock-still, except for blinking at the sun, felt his heart beating, the rhythm of his breath going in and out. How long would this last? Claire was strolling around under the linden trees, farther away. It looked like she had forgotten him . . .

Careful not to open his lips too far: "Claire!"

She continued her walk beneath the shady trees, but she did reply, "Yes?"

"Much longer?"

"No."

Silent again. Insects buzzing again. Dishes clattering inside.

" . . . longer?"

"Wolfgang?"

"Hmm?"

From quite a distance away: "You can come now! I didn't turn it on!" Bright laughter.

"What the—"

"So still was you a-standin'!"

Ha ha! Like from a bell, laughter rang from her mouth, raucous and bold.

But he caught her.

After the meal, Claire had to lie down for a nap. They stretched out under the glaring sun in a meadow, over which the air trembled in the midday heat. Silence . . .

"Wolfie?"

"Claire?"

"Will ya tell me?"

"What?"

"What's in the package . . . ?"

"Go to sleep!"

Her snoring was so loud that it scared the crickets into silence.

"Pssst!"

"You said so, I should. Never not is it right. Boo!"

Quiet again.

As if to herself: "I thought, when you told me, I'd like it better here. How come? I'm curious; all women are . . . I'd just like to say, I don't want to know at all, I couldn't care less."

"That's what you need."

"How so?"

"Just a thought."

"Wolfie?"

"Claire?"

"Is it somethin' to eats in there, or . . . ?"

But he did not respond anymore. They slept. And when they awoke—she tickled him awake—Claire stood up, smoothed her skirt, and her first words were, "Curious I is—not. But I jus' wanna know what's inside," and she thought long and hard without figuring it out. (She didn't ever find out—the package got left behind when they left the hotel.)

They spent the afternoon lying in a boat. The sky was clear; summer lent its heat one more time.

This is the last of our three days! But I'm just as happy as I was on the first. Young, full of vigor, a few brilliant days in a row—that will never happen again! Spread the happiness! We're making memories that emit sparks! Everything's ahead of us—today! Let the dead shake their fists in their graves and the unborn smile—we are! Let everyone rejoice! Fighting, but with joy! Buckling down, but with laughter! Girls, what burdens are you dragging around on such heavy chains? Shake them off. They're so light! They're hollow! Dance! Dance!

Someone called to them from the shore, a girl with

*Kurt-Tucholsky-Strasse in the city of Rheinsberg today,
a quaint street, leading to the lake.*

braided buns on both sides of her head and black, serious eyes. Her demeanor was somehow blue and gray. They rowed over to her. Which way to the forester's lodge? Was it far? They had it in mind to go there themselves, if she'd like . . . ? She thanked them and accepted.

It turned out that she also studied the field of medicine and also moved in intellectual circles. She invited poor children to meals in order to determine the effect of certain hydrates using measured portions; she also took in these victims of the capitalist economy and supported them with good advice. She explained this calmly and matter-of-factly, but firmly. The conversation coasted along. No, she was not interested in marriage just yet; she had yet to find anyone who was a man but not a sexual animal. She had a bad complexion, and it looked like she rarely bathed. Had she never been in love? Oh, she had plenty of emotional passion, she could say without boasting. She had recently drunk something at a society function that, judging by the taste, might have been Swedish punch. But that was all irrelevant. For her—the boat rocked a little then—for her there was only her duty. Her duty to give her all to her career as a scientist and a member of society.

So much for her. And her companions? To whom did she owe the pleasure? She was Aachner, Lissy Aachner, medical student. And the friendlies who had taken her along? Claire jumped in (filling Wolfgang with dread): Well, they had a little property in the area, not very significant, about 300 acres, yes, and this was her brother; they'd never been to a big city, because their parents had never allowed it, no . . . what was it like in Berlin? They had imagined it so vividly, but . . . right? Books can't really convey . . .

Student Aachner confirmed this. No, books couldn't really convey what it was like. One really must . . . she highly recommended it to them! The diverse circles, the stimulation, one really had to be on top of things, to meet all of the challenges! Well, she, Lissy Aachner, was on top of things, she could say. And it turned out that this talented girl had clear, definite, unshakable notions about everything, such as love and life. She was a monist. What was that? Social courtesy won out over a slight smile. She was filled with the conviction that everything was established on a natural basis subject to relevant circumstances. She laid particular emphasis on the circumstances, on which everything depended . . . Everything could be derived from them. She, Lissy Aachner, would never have become what she was if the circumstances and what was commonly referred to as the social environment hadn't made her a product of this new age. And knowing these circumstances, Medical Student Aachner continued, was key . . . Knowledge, that was the word! Where would it lead if we were stuck at the level of ancient barbarians and perceived rain, for example, as something divine? Rain was simply precipitation of atmospheric moisture in the form of drops or streams of water. No room for argument here. Rain was, in fact, just precipitation of atmospheric moisture in the form of drops or streams of water. And wasn't there a similar explanation for intellectual matters? Was knowledge not the basis of everything in life, too? How could you protect yourself from the pain of love without the ability to analyze the elements of the affect, love and pain? Admittedly there were exceptions, the speaker noted, but if we had not yet reached the point of knowing everything, it was due to a deficiency of our instruments or organs. We would get there eventually. Weren't religion and art also things that only a fundamentalist would consider it bold to break up into their constituent parts? Indeed, all of life itself . . . But at that point, the boat ran ashore, scraping the sandy bottom. They had arrived. Medical Student Aachner expressed her gratitude and strode through the vegetation toward the forester's lodge, a masculine stride, straight and somehow cloaked in blue and gray . . .

The pair drifted away; the boat rocked with the movement of their laughter. And once again the current carried them along, the wind sent ripples across the water, brought fresher air . . . Claire laid her hand on the edge of the boat, her bony and slightly masculine hand with the pale blue veins stretched across the back; the long, woodcarved fingers, though, lent the impression that it was an experienced hand. Those fingertips were aware of the effect of their tenderness, the joints moved with strength and assurance . . . Her hand dangled in the water, dragging a whirling stripe. The shore was far behind them, dark green and distinct.

What a dazzling day! Being there, existing without presuppositions and continually knowing that there's a woman who feels the same, thinks the same . . . (Does she really think, feel? But isn't it all the same when we just believe?) Maybe we just believe that we never meet because we're running after the same goal, side by side, striving equally, parallel . . . Knowing this is happiness. A glance to the side is all it takes; all of your perceptions are there all over again, just clad in the allure of the other. Why keep speaking? We know anyway. Why reassure, emphasize? We know, we know. And the experience and I and she—that has a ring to it, a nice triad.

And then there were just two hours left before their departure.

"Wolfgang?"

"Claire?"

"Shall we take a little walk? Come on, into the Bohemian woods!"

And they walked through the dusky park in which the stands of trees cast dark, inky shadows . . . The afternoon sky had been bright and clear—it still spanned from east to west like an enormous arch, but now it had taken on a dark hue; it was almost black, and white dots of clouds rushed by beneath it.

Surely the wind always whooshed through the treetops, swept through the trunks, set the leaves to rustling . . . It felt like a send-off. They had to leave. Quiet grief . . . they inhaled the pure air one last time. Farewell. A new stage. But we lived this one.

The path led up a hill, through fields and past blackish shrubs. They did not say anything. The bright windows of a villa gleamed high above them. Sounds? There was music up there. They walked uphill. Stood still in the dark. The yellow light did not reach them. It shone upon a few branches in the linden trees that were planted around the house. Was it a ball?

A waltz began. The violins—it must have been a large ensemble—floated sweetly by, singing the simple, delightful theme in long bow strokes. Fell silent. But then all of the instruments took up the theme, *forte*, and it was as if tender secrets were brought to light. The *piano* passages conjured up melancholy. Yet even so, it wavered, and the rhythm, the swaying, insistent rhythm darted and wooed. They stood restless, holding each other's hands, leaning . . . And then gaiety came crackling through, in a thousand tiny eighth notes, jingling like glittering glass shards falling on metal; the violins rejoiced and giggled, the basses rumbled in the depths, fat and amused, and even the cornetti player made no bones about the fact that the whole thing pleased him immensely. The part repeated; the violins climbed back up to dizzying heights once more, looked at the world from their high soprano, and finally the notes dissolved in a

*Rheinsberg Castle today: the back part of the garden (above),
and the front entrance to the renovated castle (below).*

dainty, playful manner into nothing. Was that the boom of three kettledrums? A dominant chord sounded: a sprint from the flute brought intrigue, suspense . . . And another spring, followed by the violins; the melody stopped with a new dominant chord . . . pause . . . And the sweet old theme returned with the violins, evoking memory, furtive joy, and all of the amorous whispering in the world! And then it seized the pair, and they turned slowly, floating, and they danced on the scrubby lawn, without speaking, softly at first, then faster and faster . . . Fanfares blasted the theme one more time, royal and proud, barely recognizable, and the pair twirled down the slope, dancing.

And returned to the hotel and packed their things, rode in the hotel's bumpy carriage to the train station, boarded the express train in Löwenberg, and rode through the night, effervescent and agitated, to Berlin.

To the big city, where there were troubles for them again, gray days and wistful telephone conversations, secretive afternoons, work, and the entire happiness of their great love.

*The Hotel Furstenhof today. Since the couple stayed there, the building has fallen into disrepair. It is scheduled for renovation, however, and will house condominiums.*

*Tucholsky as an eighteen-year-old in Berlin, in 1908.*

# Carnival in Berlin

## Theobald Tiger (Kurt Tucholsky)
## *Die Schaubühne*, February 12, 1914

Now the Berliner spits in his hand
and gets to work on having a ball,
slaving away from start to end
throughout this time of Carnival.

Suddenly a call from the heights
of cosmopolitan elegance
along the Spree and canals, delights,
"Put on your escarpins and dance!"

This mood, indeed, this very Muse,
naturally all men does stain;
the hand, by day to satin used,
casually beckons for champagne.

In her own way, the lady carnivals,
license granted once each year,
smooching strictly in closed circles,
when all competition is far from here.

The bourgois soul is infected too,
and keeps the dark beer flowing,
joyfully hollering, "Yahoo!"
bag o'er head in colors glowing.

What even wise men hold more dear
than thoughts sublime is wine!
Thus filled, he goes to see his Claire,
Berlin dins, he smiles. . .
To thee be thine.

# On Vacation

## Theobald Tiger (Kurt Tucholsky)
## *Die Schaubühne*, June 28, 1917

The capital!
Goo'day, oh great metropolis!
And there's the Alexanderplatz . . .
My hanky, if you please, what bliss!
My heart's a-thumpin', pitterpats.
Good ol' Spree with your patient spine,
Rowing clubs and mamsells in line,
I see you're mighty dirty within
Berlin!

Click goes the switch; the train whizzes past
The halls, the fat cathedral 'long the way.
Ugh! That Friedrichstrasse really is first-class,
An apple tree greening up at the Charité.
The people on the street do not lack:
Counts and barons all, by their walk.
Smells like money. Kickbacks, man, dive in!
Berlin!

Charlottenburg. There's my lanky Claire,
Love-child bastard by the hand, I'd say.
Though rationing on us begins to wear,
The skeleton holds all enemies at bay.
A proper reunion party that will be!
Eggs in my backpack, five and seventy.
The train is stopping! Our tribulations fleein' . . .
Berlin! Berlin!

# The Poor Woman

## Theobald Tiger (Kurt Tucholsky)
## *Die Weltbühne*, November 21, 1918

My husband? My fat man, the bard?
Dear God, now you be still!
A Don Juan? Decent, working hard
Bourgeois—in accordance with God's will.

Within those slender volumes, there . . .
How many women's kisses did he acquire;
Of silken scarves and even silkier hair,
Lust, titillation, rutting, and desire . . .

Dispense, dear sisters, with letters in number,
And that anonymous floral bequest!
They only serve to interrupt his slumber.
The fatty spends most of his time at rest.

He's lazy, flabby, and so gluttonous,
And indignant by his very nature,
All the while glugging crapulous
Red wine, at the right temperature.

I see you growing wilder, more alarmed
From day to day—oh, let it go!
My husband? My fat man, the bard?
In books: yes.
In life: no.

# To the Woman of Berlin

## Theobald Tiger (Kurt Tucholsky)
### *Die Weltbühne*, March 23, 1922

Girl, no Casanova
would ever impress you.
Could some daft lover's
fantasy really prove true?
If love-vanquished Romeo
were to sing with nostrils flared,
you would softly whisper,
"Are you whacked in the head?"
When it's romance you're wanting,
a movie you'll take in . . .
You're Mother's bestest darling,
you, woman of Berlin!


Spree-River Venus, how busy
your love, so punctual you!
Flirting until twelve-thirty,
kissing till the wee hour of two.
Dispatching all things like a pro,
your oath of love well met,
all tidy, clean, and factual:
You're a living file cabinet!
No matter how hard he presses
you to him, you won't give in.
Indeed, you're Mother's bestest,
you, woman of Berlin!

Weekdays you employ, we know,
gladly ruler and needle.
But on Sundays the stars do glow,
so Prussianly sentimental.
Thinking of that
moleskin stole,
your boyfriend bought for you?
Film star Pola's[*] shining example,
draped like she, you shimmy, too.
As you simply age, the rest
will whither with the years.
No need for swanky gestures!
For you are darling Mother's best,
sweet woman of Berlin![**]

---

[*] Pola Negri, a Polish-born dancer and silent-film star in Berlin, famous for *femme fatale* roles. In 1922, she became the first continental European star to move to Hollywood.

[**] Tucholsky wrote this poem two years after he married Else Weil.

## Prolog und kleiner Vorwurf

Hier steht es nun drin aufgemalen,
wie einzeln und im Essentialen
ich, Kögen T. mit ihr, C.P.,
gar oftens harmonieretee – –

Sagt man gewisses, nun — es rächt sich:
sieh Seite acht- und neunundsechzig —
„sie" meint man, und man spricht vom . . . Laub  . . .
nur mancher ist ein bischen taub.

Von allen hellen, blauen Tagen
ist nun mal weiter nichts zu sagen: – –
Du weißt es nicht. Die Luft . . . die See  . . .
und Du, C.P.,
und Du! C.P.!  . . .

## Prologue and a Small Reproach

Here within you'll find the portrayal
Of how essentially and in detail
I, Kögen T. with her, C.P.
So often harmonizetee—

Say certain things, revenge is mine:
See pages sixty-eight and -nine—
"she" is meant, and the word is . . . leaf . . .
Although some are a little deaf.

Of all of those bright blue days
There's really nothing more to say:
You don't know. The air . . . the sea . . .
And you, C.P.,
And you! C.P.!

*Tucholsky wrote this poem and left it as a handwritten note
in the armoire in their room in Rheinsberg.
Transcript and translation at left.
C. P. stands for Claire Pimbusch, Tucholsky's nickname for Else
Weil. Kögen T. stands for Kurt Tucholsky.*

*Kurt Tucholsky in 1920, the year he married Else Weil.*

# Among City Wizards

## Kurt Tucholsky
### *Die Weltbühne,* October 3, 1918

CHIEF MUNICIPAL Wizard Jakob Gischtschiner was drinking his morning coffee. He was apparently in a good mood— from within the thick cloud of tobacco smoke that surrounded his head there emerged a melodious whistle. Not only had he received a bonus of one hundred twenty-five talers, but his own face was looking out at him from the illustrated insert of his favorite newspaper, and that always makes a good man happy. Yes, indeed—that's how he looked, pictured there in "Our Contemporaries XXVII" in the *Berliner Guckkasten:* seated at the table in his laboratory, casual yet serious, pondering the little white book in his hand. Dozens of bottles glittered behind him, and a row of magic wands lay on black velvet before him, neat and tidy, including the one he'd received from the Shah of Persia. It was a beautiful photo. Jakob Gischtschiner smiled, as he read the accompanying text over and over again:

"Pictured here is Chief Municipal Wizard Gischtschiner, who has served the City of Berlin since 1912. From 1899 to 1911, he held the position of City Wizard in Gnesen; prior to that, he was assistant to one of the seven papal firebugs. Chief Municipal Wizard Gischtschiner is forty-eight years old; he has a son and a daughter and currently possesses fourteen artificial children, seven of which have plumbing."

Every last bit was accurate. Aurora would be quite

pleased . . . A shadow passed over the master's bearded face. Today was Sunday, which meant family, coffee klatsch, noise, and, to top off the whole spectacle, the committee meeting at City Hall at 6 o'clock. Dear God! Let it be evening—and soon!

"Come in!" the Chief Municipal Wizard said. No one came in. That must be Zebedaeus again, he thought. Aurora is absolutely right; I really should clean this place up; there's too much Krupp-crap cluttering up the apartment!

The truth of the matter was that Jakob Gischtschiner was rather absent-minded. He often forgot to unconjure his magical creations, an easy enough task for him—so everything piled up, which is why there was currently a small mob in the Gischtschiner home, created during one of his moods and bound and determined not to waste precious time doing nothing. The worst of them was Zebedaeus, Zippi for short, a small Saxon devil with a wooden head. Gischtschiner had created it eight days ago, for his children's amusement—yes, that had been a Sunday, too, and they had feasted on good food—and the thing was still running around.

"Come in!" he said, this time louder. A soft, ethereal sound reverberated throughout the room. For when Gischtschiner's doors opened, a hook on the upper edge strummed a suspended zither, eliciting a sweet sound. In this manner, strangers who entered were always somewhat enchanted by the soft harmony, as if on angels' wings. It took a lot of energy to make loud sounds here. "Well?" A group entered the room. The "Dairy Cow" was in the lead, an especially melancholy creature on two legs, thin, yellow, and unbelievably tall, with horns and an animal face, short-cropped fur, and roller skates under its feet. Then came "Anton the Fire Giant," who hadn't lit up yet, though a couple of logs glimmered and smoked in his open head. Behind them were the seven hygienic children, mostly girls, with nothing conspicious about them. The running lamp was next, followed by strange creepy-crawly things, the kind Mr. Gischtschiner liked to make when he'd eaten too many dumplings—and last of all, modest and festively dressed: Zippi.

Zippi was an utterly despicable rascal, just one meter tall, but well proportioned. At the moment, he was trying to straighten his tie. He wore a tuxedo, a petal-white shirt front, a shiny watch fob, and a black tie, but he had it all on backward. Looking at him had a dizzying effect. Where front and back were he had wickedly concealed. He looked as if some celestial fist had screwed his head down onto his neck. And he had a way of shaking his head back and forth so that everything rattled inside, winking his left eye, and screeching, "Miss! Psst! You—Miss!" He'd taught himself to do that; Mr. Gischtschiner was rather refined, so Zippi certainly hadn't learned it from him.

Zippi greeted his lord and master with the words that had been put in his mouth at the time of his creation: "Well, it's about time!" His cry had already alarmed the landlord once. Mr. Gischtschiner stood up and commanded, "Rehem!" But it was already too late.

The door opened once more; the celestial triad rang out and faded plaintively; and there in the doorway, wrapped in a simple housecoat for practical housework, stood Aurora. Aurora Gischtschiner, née Bellachini.

"Koby!" Mrs. Aurora said. Nothing more. Just "Koby!" Followed by the sound of rolling thunder. Frightened, the master and the rest of the gang crowded into a corner. It began pouring down rain.

"How many times have I told you not to leave everything lying around! Do I have a husband, or don't I have a husband? I can't go anywhere without tripping over your ridiculous things! A true civil servant should be above such behavior! I'll tell the men on the council—I most certainly will! What a fine boss you've got there, I'll tell them!"

The Chief Wizard began to beseech his wife. "Oh, no you don't!" she shouted. "You lazy bum! You good-for-nothing clown! You scoundrel!"

"I'll poof them away this instant," said the Chief Wizard.

"Oof!" cried Mrs. Aurora. For as soon as he'd mentioned poofing, Zebedaeus scurried under Mrs. Aurora, not around her, and out the door. Then all hell broke loose.

"You'll poof them away? You weakling!" she mocked. "There, the worst culprit is gone, and this isn't even all of them. The tall one that's always juggling his glass eyes is in the pantry by the canned apples, with that living rhyming dictionary. Minna already has enough to do—the girl is new and must be trained. And you're not helping a bit! At least poof these out here! On the double!"

Mr. Gischtschiner grabbed a dark blue magic wand with a silver privative alpha. "Pfffffffffft!" he said. And lo and behold, the whole gang shriveled up, lost its color, and receded. "Pfffft!" he said again, and they were all gone. With a sigh, Mrs. Aurora plopped down onto a chair. "That man—ach! What an unhappy woman I am!" Loose wisps of hair formed a veil around her pain.

Gischtschiner did not feel well. He wanted to tiptoe quietly out the door to escape, just like Zebedaeus.

She wiped her nose energetically. "Koby!" she said. "Go and straighten everything up around here! Mama's coming for lunch, and then the Merlins, Mr. Obermeier—the Dalai Lama candidate—and his wife, and I also invited that young Pfefferström, you know, the one who's interested in Katie. In spite of his pimples, he's a sweet, rich man. Dear God, the veal—you'll take care of everything, won't you, Koby?"

She was entirely back in the picture again. That's how she

was—full of rage one minute, but ready to reconcile the next—it was impossible to stay angry with her.

Full of foreboding, Mr. Gischtschiner got to work. He started with the bathroom, where he heard water running and stifled moaning. Oh, dear God! There lay Karl the Fat, a bit of historic fun: there had been no picture of this particular ruler in the encyclopedia, and Franz's tutor needed him for show-and-tell . . . so there lay Karl the Fat in the bathtub, with water streaming into his mouth. His crown and scepter were riding the waves. Gischtschiner turned off the faucet and tried to lift the prince out of the tub— what a shame, he should have come sooner! The water had splashed so much that his skin couldn't take it anymore, so there was no point in poofing him away. He was already gone. But who had done this? It couldn't have been the little grass-covered pig that was slowly climbing up the wall; he poofed that away in an angry huff. Nor the mirror bugs, either. It was Zebedaeus. Just wait!

He wasn't able to find him. He found everything else, because he was tidying everything up. He even climbed up to the attic. He found things he'd been looking for forever— like needles in haystacks and the morphing wig. He found a high C for a size-4 larynx and red and green balls that climbed up and down in one quiet corner—but he could not find Zebedaeus. He came across creatures he could barely recall—while poofing them away, he tried to remember where, when, and under what circumstances he had created them.

"Yes, yes, that was then, right . . ." he murmured pensively, and poofed the musical photo album away, the key to which he carried on his watch fob. It was the result of a delightful men's night out—Mrs. Aurora really didn't need to look inside . . . Even "Strike" turned up this time, that thing with bowling pins for legs that made such a good paperweight. And lying there on the floor were the old magic books from his school days—it always feels strange when an old man rediscovers undisturbed evidence of his youth. Wistfully he read the clumsy, childish handwriting: "Abra-ca-dabra" it spelled out, followed by a lopsided pentagram. He couldn't bring himself to poof that away; lovingly, he stroked the blue-spotted paper cover and carefully tucked the book in his pocket.

Zippi had completely disappeared. But there were traces of him. Gischtschiner's trained magic eye immediately discovered some of his monkey business here and there. In one room, all of the flies had been painted yellow, and in another, the mirror didn't work anymore—but there was no sign of the culprit. Well, at least now there was order again, and Mr. Jakob Gischtschiner was in a really good mood when he changed into his black robe for lunch. Aurora would be pleased with him—now the guests could come.

And they came. Mrs. Merlin in a wonderful chameleon dress that reflected every color, to match whatever background was behind her. Mr. Merlin in a long robe and pointy magician's hat embroidered with yellow snakes. Mrs. Obermeier, who had dressed in bourgeois fashion, was on the verge of exploding.

They came, greeted each other sugar-sweetly, and soon found themselves in the most heated discussions—the men talking shop, the women gossip. Except there were two who did not talk about the new Indian magic spells that the City of Berlin wanted to buy, nor about the third "chamber maid" the old Rübezahl had already taken on (it was quite a scandal, by the way—a man of his years!)—no, these two gazed into each others' eyes more than they spoke about anything.

The Chief Municipal Wizard's daughter was not only a good catch; she was also a pretty child. She had slightly slanted eyes with puffy lids—she almost looked Japanese.

But she was indeed pretty, and so wellread. Deputy Wizard Pfefferström, on the other hand, the youngest assistant in the Municipal Department of Magic and Administrative Conjuring, was a fat, animated young man who asked everybody everything, said everything, and knew everything.

There was just one thing he didn't know much about. Women remained a sweet mystery to him. On one occasion, he had asked a young woman, who was about to give birth, when she thought she'd marry—he also conjured up a beautiful jasper bouquet with a polite note on the day her baby boy was born, but it did nothing to change the scandalous situation. Now he was sitting across a small, decorative table from Katie, staring awkwardly at the floor in front of him.

Everyone sat down at the table, and the magnificent meal began—the soup was hot, and tiny winged cherubs puffed up their cheeks and blew on the thick, oily liquid. The bread basket stumbled around among the plates and offered his goods to anyone who would take some. On the chandelier above them, a june bug quartet merrily fiddled a little dinner music.

The second course, a nutritious sorrel dish, was delicious and received praise from all around. The ladies discussed the recipe, everyone ate some mild fish, and Mrs. Gischtschiner was just about to carve up the juicy veal when Minna burst through the door, her face beet red, eyes full of tears—and who was that, hanging on her skirt? Zippi.

He winked his left eye, tossed his wooden head back with a rattle, and cried, "Psst! You! Missy!"

"Pfooey!" the women around the table said. Mrs. Aurora glanced quickly at the Chief Municipal Wizard, who scrunched down in his chair.

"Oh, sir," Minna wailed. "This rascal keeps pestering me. I've already burned two om'lays! He annoys me and says really mean things. Down!" she said to the little one. Zebedaeus had climbed onto a chair and begun to sing:

*Those who know me*
*know that I'm abstinent,*
*from early morn' till nine at night!*
*Not a single dame exists, that . . .*

"Do you see that? Do your hear that? No, I can't stay in a house like this even one more minute!" Minna shouted indignantly.

The Chief Wizard was just about to get up and go to his work cabinet, but before he could, old fat Pfefferström whipped a folding magic wand out of his shirt pocket—he carried folding things everywhere he went—and aimed it at Zippi. Who'd begun to shriek:

"It's about ti—" Poof—he was gone.

And then something strange happened. As Pfefferström was returning to his seat, where so much food was waiting for him, and as everyone surged toward him to thank him for his presence of mind, Katie flung herself upon him and kissed him, before he saw it coming. "Papa, Mama," she cried, "You must allow us to become husband and wife!"

Their surprise was infinite. Mrs. Aurora was rather proud of her daughter, and Mr. Gischtschiner, happy for the distraction, sent a little train down to the cellar to bring up some champagne; the Obermeiers were pleased about the engagement and the champagne, and the Merlins were pleased about the engagement, the champagne, and the Obermeiers. Minna even dried her tears and brought out the crepes and coffee.

Things got really cosy. The ladies sipped sweet liqueur. Luminescent will-o'-the-wisps frolicked around, without burning the good rug, and the men lit cigars; the wheezing little train fetched the hostess's key ring. Old Mother Bellachini told stories from her childhood, of the time she spent at the fairies' boarding school, of her grandfather, who had magicked way back under Old Fritz,[*] and everyone listened in awe. Then the youngest Merlin's mother drew him into the spotlight. "Hey, Sweetiepie," she said. "Show your uncle and auntie that trick with the balls! Hmm?" The child opened his mouth excruciatingly slowly, tapped himself lightly on the back of the head, and a red billard ball rolled out, and another, and another. There was a round of applause.

"Such a good and talented boy!" Flattered, Papa Merlin smiled through his smooth, gray beard; Mama Merlin beamed, and even the betrothed couple looked on with joy.

"Take that as an example, Franz!" Mrs. Aurora said to her son, who couldn't manage any magic beyond sticking his unhappy tutor to his chair. Franz pouted.

The men smoked, the women chatted, the betrothed couple smiled and held hands. Time passed by. "I'm five o'clock," the walnut wall clock exclaimed, and cleared its throat.

"Ladies and gentlemen," the Chief Municipal Wizard got up. "I'm terribly sorry, but duty calls. Don't bother to get up; I must go to City Hall, to conjure up some taxes!" he said, and stuck his top hat on his head. Cheerful good byes ensued, with handshakes and renewed wishes for luck and blessings.

Minna sat out in the kitchen, gazing dreamily into the fire in the hearth. "Actually," she declared, "I'm a little sad. He had a great big trap and a wooden head—but he was a man!"

---

[*] "Old Fritz" is the nickname for Prussian king Frederick the Great, 1712–1786.

*Else Weil in an undated photo, likely, around 1912–1917.*

# Afterword:
# Kurt Tucholsky and Else Weil:
# A Modern Berlin Couple

## Peter Böthig, Ph. D., director of the Kurt Tucholsky Museum, Rheinsberg, Germany

Kurt Tucholsky remains unforgotten in Berlin today. Born in 1890, the journalist, satirist, poet, cabaretteur, songwriter, sometime editor of the weekly paper *Die Weltbühne*, and social critic in the tradition of Heinrich Heine was one of the most influential authors during the Weimar Republic. Tucholsky, who also wrote under four pseudonyms—Theobald Tiger, Peter Panter, Kaspar Hauser, and Ignaz Wrobel—was a socialist and pacifist who sounded an early warning against the growing might of the political right and the threat of National Socialism. In 1935, at forty-five years of age, on the run like so many of his friends and colleagues, he took his life in exile in Sweden.

But it all began much differently. Tucholsky rose to fame with his first book, *Rheinsberg. A Storybook for Lovers*. The novella came out in 1912, shortly before World War I, but it seemed to herald the modern age. Tucholsky even marketed the book in a modern way: in February 1913, he sent one of a special run of only thirty copies to Hermann Hesse and Rainer Maria Rilke (two years ago, our museum was able to obtain copy number one with a dedication to 'Claire'). And when he and his illustrator Kurt Szafranski opened a "Book Bar" on Berlin's Kurfürstendamm to sell his *Rheinsberg* and garner some media attention, he staged the spectacle just a few yards from the famous Café des Westens (commonly referred to as Café Megalomania), in which the literary avantgarde surrounding Else Lasker-Schüler and Herwarth Walden were in residence.

"It was the *Sorrows of Young Werther* for the generation dragged into the First World War. We all sent it along with our boys in the war," said fellow author Gabriele Tergit, comparing the short story with Goethe's famous first novel. With Tucholsky's book, the audience did not have to suffer along as it did with Werther, but took delight in the freshness and irreverent spirit. There was a cheerful rebellion among the youth—"Dance, dance!"—against repressive conventions, against the nationalistic Friedrich cult, against the Wilhelmine bourgeois world, urgeoning with aging mildew, which yearned for war as a "cleansing storm" over its own degeneracy.

Tucholsky, or "Wolfie's" as he calls himself in *Rheinsberg*, became famous. Much less well known, however, is the prototype for the character Claire, Claire Pimbusch, as Tucholsky named her after a character in a Heinrich Mann novel. The woman who accompanied him to the dreamy Brandenburgian village was Else Weil. Just like in this successful little book, the fascinating young woman represents in reality, too, the new aspiration for emancipation.

Else Weil was born in 1889, the eldest of three children, to Jewish parents in Berlin. After completing her college preparatory exams, she began medical studies in 1910 at the Royal Friedrich Wilhelms University in Berlin, known today as Humboldt University. This was remarkable, in that Prussia first accepted women into universities in 1908, the last German state to do so. Else Weil, therefore, was one of the first female medical students in Prussia and one of the first women to succeed in becoming licensed to practice medicine. In 1917, she received her doctor's license and earned the degree of doctor of medicine. She owned her own practice and also worked in the hospital. Two of her articles remain from the 1920s, both published in *Die Weltbühne,* in which she discussed the social issues she encountered in her daily life as a female doctor in Berlin.

Tucholsky liked Else Weil's self-confidence and unusually modern style, and they married in 1920. She took the name Tucholsky-Weil and continued to work as a physician despite being married, which was uncommon for women at the time. The marriage did not last, however. After four years, she had grown tired of her husband's love of other women and separated from him. Even after the divorce, though, the two continued to be in touch, and she remained attentive to his aches and pains.

Else Weil practiced medicine into the 1930s, with some interruptions. After the Nazis seized power and Tucholsky's books were burned at the Opernplatz, Else dropped the name Tucholsky. Because she was Jewish, her license to practice medicine was revoked in December 1933. To make ends meet, she worked as a secretary and nanny for friends in Berlin. In 1938, she went to the Netherlands, hoping to relocate there, but she was not allowed to stay. In October, Else Weil decided to emigrate to France. At first she lived in Paris, where she also worked as a nanny. It was there that she met Friedrich Epstein, a physician who had fled Berlin in 1933 and was also Jewish. The two became a couple. He called her "Pimbusch," the nickname Tucholsky had given her.

In 1940, however, the couple fled the advancing Wehrmacht to an unoccupied area in southern France, to Aix-en-Provence. She was captured and sent to the Gurs internment camp in the Pyrenees, where Hannah Arendt and Marta Feuchtwanger were also held. She was set free and lived with Epstein in Saint Cyr-sur-Mer in southern France, like many German Jewish authors. Both tried to obtain a visa for England or America, without success.

One of 23,000 stateless Jews, Else was soon captured during a raid, arrested by French authorities, and delivered to the German occupying forces (as Epstein also was sometime later). In September 1942, a transport left the Du Bourget/Drancy station in northeastern Paris every other day, headed for Auschwitz. More than thousand Jews were packed together in the railway cars, including over a hundred children. Else Weil is number 49 on the transport list for September 9, 1942: "Weil, Else, June 19, 1889, Berlin, ex-German, physician." This is the last trace of Else Weil. Either she died during transport or in the gas chamber.

A 1997 entry in the guestbook at the Kurt Tucholsky Literature Museum brought us back on the trail of Else Weil: "A niece related by marriage had really looked forward to the exhibition and was not disappointed. Gabriele Weil, London." The niece by marriage, who had not been discovered by Tucholsky researchers, was tracked down. Though a great deal of Else Weil's estate disappeared during her 1938 emigration, the niece still had many documents in her possession. During a visit in London in summer 2008, Gabriele Weil donated to the museum about fifty extremely rare documents from her family's history. These included two photographs of a young Else Weil—the first photos known of her. This material formed the foundation on which we were able to reconstruct the background and life of Else Weil.

The museum offices became a detective agency. We delved into a time long past, a stranger's family, someone else's life. First we documented the available information and established connections; then we searched through archives, estates, dusty files, yellowed paper—a search for names, places, and dates associated with Else Weil.

Today, the museum holds documents ranging from the citizenship certificate of Else's great-grandfather, Salomon Reis, from Prenzlau, Germany, in 1824, to the last letter from Else to her brother, in September 1941. Although there are many gaps that will never be filled and uncertainties remain, the picture forming before our eyes is one of a self-confident, attractive, spirited, witty woman with engaging charisma.

Else Weil embodied a sensationally new image of women. As a physician, as a Jew, and as an emancipated woman, she represents emergence into a new era; her horrific death reminds us of the millions of victims of the Holocaust. The Kurt Tucholsky Museum in Rheinsberg remains committed to preserving and honoring not only Tucholsky's work, but also her life and memory.

*A sculpure of Tucholsky in the 1930s, at the Tucholsky Museum.*
*The title of the panel in the upper right is "Discontinued Poet."*

*Kurt Tucholsky's typewriter (above) and his desk and suitcase (below) at the Tucholsky Museum in Rheinsberg Castle.*

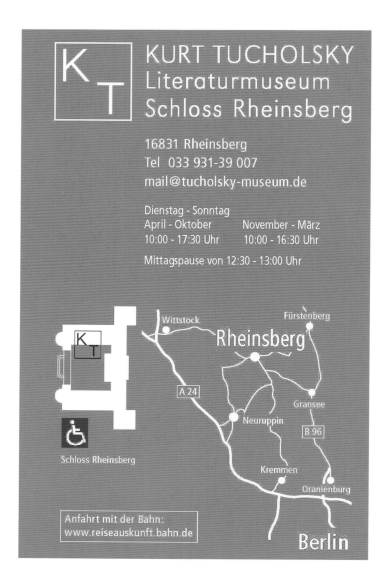

*Map to the museum in Rheinsberg Castle. The castle is about 65 miles northwest of Berlin, and accessible by train.*

Dear Reader, we hope you enjoyed this book. If you would like to visit the quaint little town of Rheinsberg now, we recommend the following places:

**MARITIM**
Hafenhotel Rheinsberg

## Explore, experience, enjoy...

...the picturesque resort town of Hafendorf Rheinsberg and the Maritim Hafenhotel Rheinsberg nestled on the southern tip of the Mecklenburg Lake District. Surrounded by Scandinavian-style half-timbered houses, the hotel's prime spot on the harbour with bathing shore and lighthouse guarantees year-round relaxation.

- 176 rooms and suites
- Accessible lighthouse with observation platform
- Lakeshore with adjoining sunbathing lawn
- Water sport provisions

- Three restaurants with terrace seating right on the harbour
- '53°/12°' nightclub
- Wellness lounge

Give us a call – we're happy to provide you with more info!

Hafendorfstrasse 1 · 16831 Rheinsberg · Germany
Phone +49 (0) 33931 800-0 · Fax +49 (0) 33931 800-888
info.rhh@maritim.com · www.maritim.com

Business premises of Wellnesshotel Hafendorf Rheinsberg GmbH & Co. KG
Biedermannweg 6 · 14052 Berlin · Germany

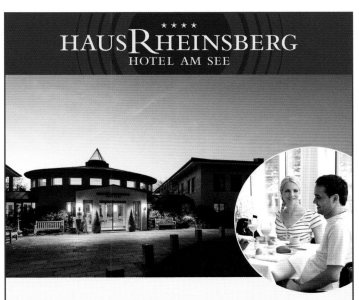

★ ★ ★ ★
# HAUS RHEINSBERG
## HOTEL AM SEE

## VACATION WITH MANY EXTRAS

Enjoy nature and culture: Experience the four-star
Haus Rheinsberg Hotel and spend a dream vacation
in the lake district of historic Ruppin County.
The hotel is wheelchair accessible. Relaxation
at its finest within a short drive from Berlin.

- Sumptuous breakfast buffet daily
- Free indoor pool and sauna year round
- Group rates available

HausRheinsberg | Hotel am See
Donnersmarckweg 1 | 16831 Rheinsberg
Phone: +49-033931-344 0 | Fax: +49-033931-344 555
post@hausrheinsberg.de | **www.hausrheinsberg.de**

 UNIQUELY BARRIER-FREE

A SUBSIDIARY OF FÜRST DONNERSMARCK-STIFTUNG

# THE
# SEEHOF
## RHEINSBERG

## THIS PRECIOUS LITTLE COUNTRY HOTEL IS A SPECIAL TREAT!

**Award-winning hotel and restaurant**

Seestraße 18 ǀ 16831 Rheinsberg
Tel.: +49 33931 403 - 0
Fax: +49 33931 403 - 99
E-Mail: **info@seehof-rheinsberg.de**
Internet: **www.seehof-rheinsberg.de**

## WWW.SEEHOF-RHEINSBERG.DE

# The Ideal

Sure, that's what you want
A *mansion in the countryside*
with a *magnificent porch*
the **Baltic Sea** in front
in back
*Friedrichstraße*
a wonderful view
*rural chic*
from the **back window**
you can see the **Alps**
—and the **movie theater**
is right around the corner
. . . sure you do . . .

# The Tucholsky Book Store in Berlin

Tucholskystraße 47
10117 Berlin-Mitte

☎ 01149-30-2757-7663
kurt@buchhandlung-
tucholsky.de
www.buchhandlung-
tucholsky.de

Mo-Sat 10am–7pm

Two blocks from S-Bahn
Oranienburger Straße

## Das Ideal

Ja, das möchste:
Eine **Villa im Grünen**
mit *großer Terrasse,*
vorn die **Ostsee,**
hinten die
**Friedrichstraße;**
mit schöner Aussicht,
*ländlich-mondän,*
vom **Badezimmer**
ist die
**Zugspitze** zu sehn –
aber abends zum **Kino**
hast dus nicht weit.
. . .
*Ja, das möchste!*
. . .

*Tucholsky-*
**Buchhandlung**

 presents

## 2010–2014 Program

available at
www.berlinica.com
www.amazon.com
www.barnesandnoble.com

**Kurt Tucholsky**
**BERLIN! BERLIN!**
*Hardcover, 198 pp., $23.95*
*ISBN: 978-1-935902-21-8*
*Softcover, 198 pp., $15.95*
*ISBN: 978-1-935902-20-1*

TUCHOLSKY'S BERLIN!
BERLIN! shines a light
on the Weimar Republic
and the Golden Twen-
ties, on the cabarets and
theaters, the city and
its denizens, politics
and street fights, and
the post-war struggle
between the militaristic
Right and the pacifistic
Left, which foreshad-
owed the Third Reich.
This book features
Tucholsky's news stories
and poems about his
home town; a glimpse
of the age that shaped
the century. This col-
lection of Berlin stories
has never been pub-
lished in America.

Mark Twain

**A TRAMP IN BERLIN**

*Hardcover, 176 pp., $22.95*
*ISBN: 978-1-935902-92-8*
*Softcover, 176 pp., $14.95*
*ISBN: 978-1-935902-93-5*

Erik Kirschbaum

**ROCKING THE WALL**

*Hardcover, 144 pp., $19.95*
*ISBN: 978-1-935902-73-7*
*Softcover 144 pp., $11.95*
*ISBN: 978-1-935902-74-4*

Andreas Nachama, Julius
Schoeps, Hermann Simon

**JEWS IN BERLIN**

*Softcover, 310 pp., $23.95*
*ISBN: 978-1-935902-60-7*

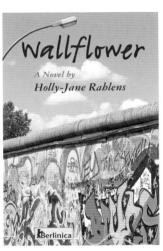

Holly-Jane Rahlens

**WALLFLOWER**

*Softcover, 150 pp., $11.95*
*ISBN: 978-1-935902-70-6*
*Ebook also available*

Michael Brettin / Peter Kroh

**BERLIN 1945. WORLD WAR II: PHOTOS OF THE AFTERMATH**

*Softcover, 220 pp., $18.95*
*ISBN: 978-1-935902-03-4*
*Preface by Stephen Kinzer*

Erik Kirschbaum

**BURNING BEETHOVEN GERMAN CULTURE IN WWI**

*Softcover, 150 pp., $13.95*
*ISBN: 978-1-935902-85-0*
*Ebook also available*

Thomas Flemming

**BERLIN IN THE COLD WAR**

*Softcover, 90 pp., $9.95*
*ISBN: 978-1-935902-80-5*
*Ebook also available*

Monika Maertens

**BERLIN FOR FREE**

*Softcover, 104 pp., $10.95*
*ISBN: 978-1-935902-40-9*
*Ebook also available*

Rose Marie Donhauser

**THE BERLIN COOKBOOK**

**TRADITIONAL RECIPES
AND NOURISHING STORIES**

*Hardcover, 96 pp., $24.95
ISBN: 978-1-935902-51-5*

*Softcover, 96 pp., $19.95
ISBN: 978-1-935902-50-8*

Lothar Heinke

**WINGS OF DESIRE
ANGELS OF BERLIN**

*Hardcover, 102 pp., $25.95
ISBN: 978-1-935902-14-0*

*Softcover, 102 pp., $16.95
ISBN: 978-1-935902-18-8*

*German edition also available*

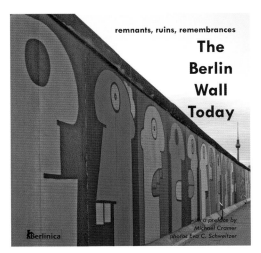

Michael Cramer

**THE BERLIN
WALL TODAY**

**REMNANTS,
RUINS,
REMEMBRANCES**

*Softcover, 86 pp.
$15.95
ISBN:
978-1-935902-102*

*German Edition
ISBN:
978-1-935902-119*

*Ebook also available*

Adrienne Haan

## BERLIN, MON AMOUR

*Music CD, 1 disc
in English or German.*

*Music from the 1920s,
by Bert Brecht, Kurt Weil,
and Friedrich Hollaender*

*48 minutes; retail $15.95*

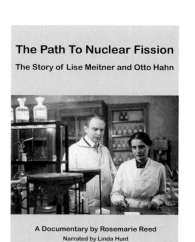

Rosemarie Reed

## THE PATH TO
## NUCLEAR FISSION

*English/German (subtitled)
Run time: 81 minutes; $19.95*

Stefan Roloff

## THE RED ORCHESTRA
## MOVIE DVD

*English/German (subtitled)
Run time: 57 minutes; $24.95*